HIDDEN PLACES

TRASH TO TREASURE COZY MYSTERIES, BOOK 6

DONNA CLANCY

SUMMER PRESCOTT BOOKS PUBLISHING

SIGN UP FOR THE SPBP NEWSLETTER

Do you love Cozy Mysteries, Freebies, Contests and always being in the know?

You'll love the Summer Prescott Books Newsletter!

Click below for the best and most up to date info. Join the fun!

Sign Up

CONTENTS

My mom instilled the love of Christmas in me when I was very young. I lost her a little over a year ago but in my mind I can still see the happiness on her face and feel the excitement she shared with everyone at the holidays.
Christmas will always be a special time of year to hold tight to the memories she created.

CHAPTER ONE

Cupston is so pretty this time of year," Gabby said, looking out the window on the way to town. "Look at the house over there. It looks like a big gingerbread house."

"Have you seen my mom's house? I don't think there is an inch on the property that isn't lit up with Christmas lights," Sage replied. "She started to decorate in October in order to be able to turn them on for the Thanksgiving Night Festival."

"I don't understand how you can say your favorite holiday is Halloween when there are beautiful lights everywhere at Christmas," Gabby said.

"To each his own, I guess. I like creepy over pretty," Sage replied. "But that's not to say I don't enjoy riding around light gazing."

"Speaking of riding around, I can't believe Cliff and his dad managed to put together a Christmas hayride at the farm. Last I heard, they weren't going to do it until next year," Gabby said.

"The Halloween Hayride did so well they were able to buy lights and decorations for it. The Christmas ride isn't as long as the Halloween one but it's nice. And the children's gift fund is going to benefit from it," Sage replied.

"Rory and I are going this weekend," Gabby said. "I'm glad they changed the dates so it ends on

December 23rd and the Fulton family can enjoy the holiday instead of working through it."

"Cliff said the money would be tallied on the last day. If we need to make any last-minute purchases for families applying for help later than the deadline, the money will be available to use."

"I don't think the Fulton family realizes how much they do for this town," Gabby stated.

"They do it because they want to, not because they want to be noticed for it."

"You got yourself a good one when it comes to Cliff," Gabby replied. "And he is crazy about you."

"I'm pretty crazy about him, too. We get along so well and have so much in common. And, what's great is he doesn't get upset over my obsession with mysteries," Sage stated.

"Have you decided what to get him for Christmas yet? It's only a week away."

"Not yet. Have you got Rory anything?"

"I found a beautiful, antique drafting set online. It is from the early 1800s and is complete in the original wood box. He's going to freak when he sees it."

"Sounds awesome. Here we are," Sage said, turning onto a long winding driveway leading to the Flemming mansion.

"I can't believe you took the old beat-up cabinet you had and returned it to its original beauty. I wish I had your vision."

"This was a fun project. I've never done anything like it before. But once I found a picture of a similar cabinet online the rest was easy. And I love the satin finish I used to seal the restored piece. It definitely belongs in a Victorian parlor," Sage said, proudly.

"The Flemmings are going to love it," Gabby replied.

"Mrs. Flemming is expecting us at six o'clock. She assured me she would have her two sons at the house to move it into the parlor and then we can get to the last meeting of the children's fund committee at the library."

"We have twenty-six people who volunteered to be there tonight to wrap gifts. We had enough money in the fund to cover every family who signed up for help this year. I'm in charge of stocking stuffing tonight," Gabby said. "You got nailed for helping to put bikes together."

"I'm hoping there will be enough guys there to take over the job and I can work on packing up what is on each families list. Cliff said he's work on the bikes along with his dad."

"I believe there were sixteen bikes requested on the applications. They were supposed to be delivered to the library today from the bike store in Moosehead."

"That's a lot of bikes to put together. I hope we have a good-sized number of men show up to volunteer," Sage said, pulling up to the front of the mansion. "Here we are and right on time."

"This place looks stunning," Gabby said. "Look at the size of the wreath over the front door. It's massive."

"I'm sure the Flemmings have a professional company come in and decorate for them. It is stunning regardless," Sage replied, climbing down out of the van.

"Sage, Gabby, how nice to see you," Mrs. Flemming said, walking down the stairs. "Do you have my cabinet with you? My husband is out so I can get it into the house and put a sheet over it to hide it until the twenty-third when I will unveil it for him."

"We do. Are your sons here?" Sage asked.

"Phillip, Stephen, please come out here and move the new cabinet into the formal parlor," she yelled into the house. "Now!"

Sage opened the rear of the van, and the two men slid the piece out. She took off the cushioned pads and they carried the piece inside.

"Be careful, boys," their mother lectured. "It's your father's Christmas present."

She requested the two friends follow her inside. Mrs. Flemming had already cleared a space where she wanted it to be placed. Her sons gingerly put the cabinet where she wanted it and then waited.

"Place the green king-sized blanket over the cabinet so your father doesn't see it from the door. I told him he couldn't come in here until the party," she said to her sons. "Then you are free to leave."

They didn't have to be told twice and scurried off as quickly as they could before she asked them to do something else. Sage and Gabby side-eyed each other.

"Robots, or what?" Gabby whispered to Sage as Mrs. Flemming walked around the cabinet to make sure it was hidden all the way around.

"It's wonderful, just like I imagined it would be," the new owner stated, clasping her hands together in delight. "I can't wait for my husband to see his new gun cabinet at our open house."

"I'm so glad you like it," Sage said, accepting the envelope her client was handing her.

"Like it, I love it. And I have a list of other projects I would like you to do for me," she replied, smiling.

"Maybe after the new year we can sit down and have a meeting and you can tell me what pieces you are looking for," Sage suggested.

"That would be perfect. The holidays get so hectic. I would like to extend an invitation to you and Gabby, and your plus ones, to come to our Christmas open house on the twenty-third so you can see for yourself the reaction people have when viewing your work. And bring business cards as I have a feeling people will be wanting you to create something for them also."

"Is the open house formal dress?" Gabby asked, hoping it wasn't because her plus one would not go if it was.

"Oh, no, my dear. It's all about having fun and celebrating the holiday. I wouldn't expect you to wear jeans and sneakers, of course. If you have something red or green, that would be nice, but above all, wear something comfortable."

"Should we bring a dish?" Sage asked.

"The whole event is catered. Just bring yourselves and maybe a canned good from each of you to benefit the Cupston Food Pantry. Last year we filled over a hundred boxes and delivered them to the pantry. It helps them get through the winter months."

"I've volunteered at the pantry. The people who run it are wonderful," Gabby stated.

"Your parents attend my party every year. It will be nice to see the next generation in attendance," Mrs. Flemming said, ushering them to the door.

"Mother!"

"I have to go. Those two can't get along to save themselves. It's frustrating. They should be out working at their age and not sitting home playing video games all day. But their father… he just looks the other way and lets them do whatever they want. I'm sorry, I shouldn't air dirty laundry. We'll see you on the twenty-third," she said, closing the door in their faces.

They stood on the steps in shock that they had been rushed out of the mansion in the fashion they were. Loud yelling could be heard coming from inside.

"I guess money doesn't buy happiness," Gabby said.

"Not here anyway," Sage agreed. "Let's get out of here before something comes flying out through a window."

"I'm right behind you."

They arrived at the Cupston Library and had a difficult time trying to find somewhere to park. They ended up in the rear parking lot, and even there, Sage had to squeeze into a spot between a cockeyed parked car and a tree.

"Wow! What a great turnout," Sage said, opening the back of the van. "What do you want to carry? Bags of bows or rolls of wrapping paper?"

"It looks like we'll have to make two trips to get everything into the library. Why don't we take the paper first and come back for the bows. That way people can begin wrapping," Gabby suggested.

"Need some help?" Sarah Fletcher asked, getting out of her car.

"I didn't see you there," her daughter said. "Yes, we could use some help."

The three women loaded up everything they could carry. There were at least thirty people already there, drinking coffee and soda. Some of the men had started putting the bikes together and LouAnn, Gabby's mom, was directing the gift sorting according to the lists of each registered family.

The paper and bows were set on the back tables which had been set up as wrapping stations. There was a box of black trash bags which the gifts would be put in after they were wrapped and labeled with a tag displaying the family's name. The library had graciously consented to leaving the gifts in the downstairs conference room until they were to be picked up on the morning of the twenty-third between nine and noon.

"People really came through this year with donations. Look at the table full of stocking stuffers," LouAnn told her daughter. "The secret sponsor

Christmas tree upstairs in the main lobby didn't have one star left on it at the end of last week."

"That's what I love about living in this small town, people taking care of people," Sarah replied. "It's been a tough year for many of our locals. At least the kids will all still have a merry Christmas."

"And Terri, the manager of the food pantry, said she has forty-two Christmas dinners to be picked up the same day, so they can come here and then go there to get their food. Everything came together so well this year," LouAnn replied.

"Speaking of the food pantry, we delivered Mrs. Flemming's cabinet to her today and she invited us to her open house. I didn't know you attended her party every year," Sage said to her mom.

"I have for the last twenty years or so. The food is to die for, and she has raffles every half hour for some pretty nice gifts. It's a lot of fun. Her donation to the food pantry is well appreciated and it fills the shelves for a good portion of the winter months."

"And if you want to buy extra raffle tickets, the money is divided between the food pantry and our children's gift fund. The event is well attended, and I've even seen a few celebrities there over the years," LouAnn stated.

"Mrs. Flemming told me to bring some of my business cards with me when I go. She seems to think once people see the Victorian cabinet I restored for her, my business doing special orders will pick up."

"I had to turn people away for appointments to do their hair for the event. Even with the three of us working full tilt, there wasn't enough available slots for everyone who wanted one. And I promised the girls we would be out of there by five o'clock as they had their own parties to go to that night," Gabby said. "I just never pictured myself attending the same event with all the well-to-dos who come in to get their hair done. Although, I have to admit it is one of the best days of the year for tips for us."

"Okay, less gabbing and more working," Cliff said, coming up behind the group and slipping his arm around Sage's waist.

"Hello, Mr. Fulton," Sage said, turning around. "Are you and your son ready to get to work?"

"Call me Pierce, please," he requested. "I put together a bike or two while Cliff was growing up. He had this bad habit of playing daredevil and destroying his bikes within a year of getting them."

"And now he has tractors to play on," Sage said, laughing.

"And thankfully, those are a lot harder to wreck," Pierce replied.

"Soda and coffee are over there, the bike area is over there," LouAnn said, pointing to the stack of boxes containing the bikes. "There should be plenty of available tools to use."

"Come on, Dad. We have lots to do," Cliff said. "Do you want coffee or a soda?"

"I'll grab a coffee. This might be a long night," he replied.

"Where is Rory tonight?" Sarah asked Gabby.

"He had to attend a meeting with the planning board. He's trying to pull permits for an addition on the old Sharp house and is running into problems."

"I heard someone bought the old place. Are they restoring it?"

"They are and also adding on almost another whole house to the original structure. It would be a huge job for Rory's construction company if the problems are ironed out with the permits," Gabby replied.

"Are they going to build over the winter months?"

"No, they already have permits for the restoration phase so they will work on the original house inside and then start the outside work in March. He's so stoked for this job, and he told me it would cover the cost of our honeymoon and some of the wedding."

"I thought your Dad was paying for your wedding?"

"He is, but you know Rory and how stubborn he is," Gabby said, pulling a soda can out of the cooler.

"There are certain things he insists on paying for and nothing my dad says to him will change his mind."

"He may soften the closer the wedding gets. Now, I am off to wrap and sort gifts. Have fun stuffing stockings," Sage replied, grabbing a soda.

By ten o'clock, all the bikes had been assembled and were standing in a line at the back of the room. When one was finished, Sage would hang a tag on the handlebars with the name of the family who would receive the bike. A large bike gift bag was then draped over the seat.

Midnight rolled around. Between lots of yawns and many cups of coffee all the gifts were wrapped, and all the stockings were stuffed. The large trash bags were filled with the gifts on each individual list and labeled with a tag. A smaller bag with the needed number of stockings for the family was set next to the trash bag.

"Job well done," Sarah said, looking at what they had accomplished.

"Another year in the books," LouAnn said. "And we even have extra gifts left over in case we have late requests come in."

"You did a great job as chairman again this year," Sarah said to LouAnn. "If you ever decide to retire we'll be lost."

"I don't think so. Look at all the new faces who showed up to volunteer this year. The Christmas spirit will never die in this town as long as we have new generations who care and by the looks of things tonight, we have nothing to worry about."

"Thank you, everyone, and Merry Christmas," Sarah said.

"I'll be here the morning of the twenty-third for pick-up. If anyone has some time off and would like to help it would be appreciated," LouAnn said. "It's only from nine to noon."

Cliff and his dad were packing up the tools used to assemble the bikes. Sage and Gabby made several trips to Sage's van removing the excess supplies not used which would be stored in Sage's attic for next year.

"We're heading out," Cliff said. "Dad and I have to be up at five for some deliveries arriving at the farm."

"Who ran the hayride tonight with you both here?" Gabby asked.

"Joel, one of our farmhands, agreed to stay and man the festivities," Cliff's dad replied.

"Rory and I will see you Friday night. We're coming to go on the hayride to see the lights and decorations. I love this time of year," Gabby said, smiling.

"We need to make plans for the holidays," Cliff stated. "Maybe at supper tomorrow night?"

"I forgot to tell you we were invited to Mrs. Flemming's open house on the twenty-third," Sage said to Cliff. "Can we go after you close the hayride?"

"The ride closes at seven. I need time to shower and change but I can pick you up at eight and we can be there by eight-thirty, if that's okay," he replied.

"Perfect. Gabby, do you and Rory want to meet at my house, and we'll all go together?"

"I'll talk to Rory and let you know. I'm heading home. I have to open the salon at eight, but I need to restock before everyone else gets there."

"Thank you for helping," her mother said, giving her a hug. "I'll see you at the open house on Sunday night."

"Are you ready to leave, Sage? Dad and I will walk you to your van," Cliff offered.

"Are we all done, Mom?"

"LouAnn and I will lock up. You go ahead and go home," Sarah said to her daughter. "Love you."

"Love you more," she replied, walking out hand in hand with Cliff.

Sage was in her shop early the next morning working on a special order which was to be a Christmas gift for one of her repeat customers, Marie

Simms, from her husband. He had found six old shutters at a yard sale held at the first house they lived in together and wanted Sage to create a room divider using them.

She had already painted the base coat on the shutters using black satin paint and was now lining them up to spray a customized mural. The couple had honeymooned in London and Ralph wanted Big Ben and London Bridge spray painted in gold across the surface of the shutters.

Sage had drawn a large outline of each structure and taped them to the shutters. She sprayed around the cutouts with gold creating black buildings at the bottom. As she moved up the shutters she sprayed a lighter and lighter coat of gold so at the top the black paint looked like a night sky with specks of gold stars.

She stepped back and checked her work. It was exactly what she pictured as a finished piece. Sage would let the paint dry overnight and apply a coat of polyurethane the following morning to seal it. Ralph would be able to pick the finished piece up the morning of the twenty-third.

All her other special orders for the holiday were finished and delivered. Sage was proud of herself as it seemed every year she was behind and was completing gifts at the last minute. Now that the shutters were just about done for Ralph, she could take the afternoon off and get some of her own holiday errands done.

She promised to meet Gabby at the Christmas tree lot in town at two o'clock. They would pick out their trees together and have their annual hot chocolate with candy canes. Sage was looking for the perfect tree this year as it was the first Christmas she and Cliff would be spending together. It would also be the first year with two cats in the house.

Most of Sage's ornaments were blown glass she collected over the years. After what she witnessed with the cats and her Halloween decorations, she knew the tree would be a huge temptation for them. Before she met Gabby at the tree lot, she was going to stop at the *Cupston Five and Dime* to purchase some plastic ornaments for the lower part of the tree in case they attacked it and pulled off the ornaments to bat around. It would be the first year since she was eighteen her ornaments would be different.

Looking back, a lot of things were different. She had a new boyfriend, two new roommates, and had solved several mysteries which had earned her a collection of diamonds and a full storage trailer for her business. It had been a good year not only for her but all those around her.

Sage checked her phone for the time and had just enough leeway to get to the store before she had to be at the tree lot. She locked up her workshop, went into the house to check on the cats, and grab her wallet. In the few hours she had been out in her shop, the cats had managed to drag some of her Christmas decorations around which she already had out around the house. The string of twinkling lights had been pulled down from around the bay window and were in a heap on the floor.

"Come on guys, give me a break," she said picking up the lights. "I have a lot of people coming over here for Christmas Eve and I want the house to look nice, but it won't if you keep destroying everything."

The cats, sitting on the couch, stared at her as she was talking to them. They laid down, stretched, and rolled over like they really didn't care what she was upset about. They continued to watch her as she reset the lights in the hooks around the window.

"Don't touch them while I'm gone," she said, wagging her finger at her roommates. "Oh, who am I kidding? You're cats and you'll do what you want to do. Maybe as you get older you'll learn to chill out at the holidays."

Cupston Five and Dime was the busiest Sage had ever seen it. With less than a week until Christmas, shoppers were filling their carts, laughing, and talking with anyone they knew. Sage grabbed a cart and headed for the tree decoration section. As she perused the boxes of ornaments she heard a commotion coming from another part of the store. What started as a disagreement had blown into a full-fledged argument.

"I know those voices," Sage said, heading for the area of the disruption.

CHAPTER TWO

Sage turned the corner of the last aisle, and her thoughts were confirmed. The two Flemming brothers were fighting over a video game they each wanted to buy.

"I saw it first," Phillip Jr. was yelling.

"But I picked it up first," Stephen replied, not letting go of the video they both had their hands on.

"I'm warning you. Let it go," Phillip said, growling at his brother.

"Or you'll what? You're a wuss. You won't do anything," Stephen said, taunting him.

"Boys, break it up," Mr. Turner, the owner of the five and dime said, reaching for the video game.

"Back off, Turner, or we'll make sure no one shops here anymore," Phillip Jr. replied.

"I don't care who your parents are, you're threats mean nothing to me," he replied, snatching the video from them. "Both of you, get out of my store and don't come back."

"You'll be sorry, old man," Phillip said, glaring at the owner as he exited the door.

"Mr. Turner, are you okay?" Sage asked.

"I'm fine. Two spoiled rotten kids who need a whack or two to straighten them out," he replied. "I'm sorry for the disruption, folks. Keep shopping, they won't be back to wreck anymore of your day."

"Has this happened before?" Sage asked.

"One other time. I threw them out, they went home and lied to their father about what happened, and he came down here in a tear. Fortunately for me, there were many witnesses who backed me up and he left here furious he had been lied to. But I would venture to say nothing came of it. He treats those two like they're still five years old. They haven't worked a day in their life and think they can do whatever they want and get away with it. It's a shame really. Their mother tries to make them grow up and be accountable for what they do but she is constantly shot down by their father."

"Well, as long as you're okay, I guess I'll finish my shopping," Sage said, turning her cart around. "Merry Christmas."

"You also, and tell your mom the same."

Sage purchased some royal blue and deep purple plastic ornaments. She decided because she was changing her ornaments and going with a color scheme, she also bought fluffy purple garland and strings of blue lights. Tinsel would be out of the question this year as she didn't want the cats to eat it. She paid for her items and left for the tree lot.

Gabby was waiting at the entrance with two hot chocolates in hand.

"Sorry, I'm late," Sage said, explaining what happened at the store as they walked around the tree lot.

"Do you know what size tree you are looking for?" Gabby asked. "I want a six-footer. Anything bigger and I'll have to take some off the top to fit in my house."

"I have tall ceilings in my living room, so I was thinking maybe an eight-foot tree. I'm having everyone over on Christmas Eve and I want the place to look really festive."

"I think the taller trees are at the back of the lot," Gabby suggested.

The two friends walked around, holding up a tree here and there, comparing the branches, and looking for any big holes where the branches had not grown. They had finished their drinks and Sage went to grab another one for each of them. She also brought back a gingerbread man cookie to go with the hot chocolate.

"That's really cute," Gabby said, holding up the cookie.

"And they smelled so good I couldn't resist," Sage replied, taking a big bite.

"No tree is perfect you know," Gabby said, finding a tree she liked. "I think I'll get this one."

She flagged the attendant down and followed him and the tree to the front where she paid for it, and he tied it to the top of her car. Gabby returned to her friend at the back of the lot where she was standing and perusing two trees standing side by side.

"I have it narrowed down to these two," Sage said. "What do you think?"

"I think they're huge," she replied, laughing. "Will they fit in your living room?"

"I believe so. I'm going to have to chop off some of the trunk to get it to fit in the tree stand which should help it to clear the ceiling."

"They both look nice," Gabby said, walking around the trees to see the front and back.

"Then again, I was looking at those over there," she said, pointing to the corner of the lot. "Those trees come in pots and can be replanted in your yard after the holidays. I thought it might look nice at the end of my driveway."

"That's a great idea," Gabby replied. "I wish I had seen those before I bought the one I did. I could have planted it next to the door of my salon."

"It's settled. I'm getting one in a pot," Sage said, walking over to the biggest one.

"That's a nice tree. It will look great in your living room if the cats don't destroy it first."

"I bought all new plastic ornaments for this year so the cats can't break any of my glass collectibles," Sage said, waving down the attendant.

"Smart thinking. I hate to cut this short, but we are overbooked at the salon, and I need to get back. It seems like everyone needs their hair done in this town to attend their holiday parties. Which I'm not complaining, mind you, it's great for business, but people have no patience this time of year. Everything is go, go, go."

"I know, so much to get done and so little time to do it."

"I talked to Rory, and we will meet you at your house on the twenty-third at eight. He said he would feel more comfortable going to a fancy gathering if he had friends to talk to while there."

"Great! I guess we will see you then," Sage said, hugging her friend goodbye.

She waited until Gabby left and then told the waiting attendant she wanted two potted trees and showed him which ones. He carried them to the front, wrapped the pots in burlap so the dirt wouldn't spill out, and loaded them into Sage's van.

Gabby is going to be so surprised to see a tree waiting at her salon door tomorrow morning when she gets to work.

Sage sat in her vehicle thinking. She still hadn't bought anything for her mom. Sarah Fletcher was one of the most difficult people to buy a gift for and Sage struggled every Christmas to find just the right gift for her mom. She had everything and if she didn't she went out and bought it for herself.

"What am I going to get her?" she said, tapping the screen of her cell phone. "She likes jewelry. Maybe I'll go poke around *All That Glitters* jewelry store and see if I can find anything."

It was difficult to find somewhere to park on Main Street as a lot of the town's locals were out Christmas shopping. Sage finally found a place to park behind the five and dime and walked to the jewelry store a few doors down. It was as busy as the rest of the shops in town and Sage had to wait her turn to be able to get up next to the display cases.

"Sage, how nice to see you again," Mrs. Flemming said, turning around to walk away from the case she was perusing. "Spending some of your well-earned money on Christmas shopping?"

"I am. I still need something for my mom. She is the worst person to buy a gift for," Sage replied. "And you? Are you Christmas shopping?"

"I try to support the local businesses when I buy the raffle gifts for my open house. Betsy Stone always has the most beautiful pieces and while I'm shopping for the raffle I manage to find a few trinkets for myself also. Lord knows, I have to do my own shopping as those lazy good for nothings I have to call sons won't buy me a single thing for Christmas. They spend every cent they get on video games."

"I'm sorry. I saw them shopping earlier and you're right, they were fighting over a video game at the five and dime."

"I'm sorry you witnessed that little scene. I made them go in and apologize to Mr. Turner. They were not happy about doing it and their father lambasted me when I took them home after the apology. He told me people should mind their own business and Mr. Turner had no right to throw his sons out of the store."

"I beg to differ. I was there and they disrupted the whole store. I have to side with Mr. Turner and what he did," Sage said firmly. "And it sounds like you agreed with it too."

"I did. If I only I could get my husband to wake up and see how he is ruining his own sons' lives. Sometimes, I think things would be so different if he wasn't around to shield them from everything and they were forced to grow up."

"I wish I had an answer for you," Sage replied.

"I don't know why I find it so easy to talk to you, but I do."

"My mom says I have the kind of aura around me which makes people feel comfortable. It's a superpower, I guess," Sage said, smiling.

"You hold on to that superpower because it is a great thing when people trust you enough to open up to you and tell you what they are feeling."

"Thank you. I guess we'll see you Sunday night. Have a great rest of the day," Sage said, moving up to the case.

"Find your mom something nice," Mrs. Flemming said, heading for the next case over. "She deserves it."

Yes, she does, but what?

Sage strolled from case to case looking for anything which would catch her eye. Her mother liked silver rather than gold. In the very last case she looked in, she found exactly what she was looking for. She waited for Mrs. Stone to finish with the customer she was waiting on and waved her over to where she was standing.

"Sage, how nice to see you," the jeweler said. "Who are we shopping for today? That handsome boyfriend of yours or your mom?"

"My mom, and I think I found just the thing. May I please see the silver ring set with the tanzanite stones?"

"I love tanzanite. The way the stones change color depending on the angle you see them is fascinating," she replied, taking the ring out of the case, and handing it to Sage.

Sage slipped the ring on her finger. The center stone was a deep blue with a hint of purple to it. The three smaller stones on either side of the main stone were lighter in color, more purple than blue, but all matched perfectly.

"My mom and I take almost the same size. If she would like can she get it sized?"

"Definitely. I know your mom loves silver and not gold. Did you see the matching sterling necklace which goes perfectly with the ring?"

"I must have missed it."

"Stay right here and I'll go get it for you," Mrs. Stone said, hurrying off to another display case. "Here it is."

"They do go nicely together. Mom would look great wearing them to one of her town meetings. I'll take both. And may I please see the royal blue star sapphire ring in the corner over there."

"This is gold. Not for your mom, I assume? Are you giving yourself a little gift this season?"

"No, I was thinking of Gabby. I don't know her ring size though so I would have to know that sizing is included in the price like with my mom's ring," Sage replied.

"Again, sizing is included."

"Great! I'll take the ring for Gabby, too," Sage said, taking out her credit card. "She's going to love it."

"You have great taste. Follow me to the register."

"Does Mrs. Flemming always do her raffle shopping in here?" Sage asked while waiting for the card to clear.

"Every year. And she doesn't care what the items cost. If something catches her eye, she buys it for the raffle. She says it's her way of giving back."

"Wow! I hope I win one of her raffles," Sage replied, smiling. "I don't know exactly what she bought but anything from here would be a treasure."

"She's not stingy by any means. Is this your first year attending her open house?"

"It is, and I'm really looking forward to it. My mom says the food is to die for and there is plenty of it."

"Your mom has been known to win a few of the raffles each year. She is very lucky in that way," Mrs. Stone said, handing Sage her purchases. "Are you sure you don't need anything for that handsome guy of yours?"

"I already have his gift, thank you. It's something he will never expect."

"I guess we will see you at the open house," the jeweler said, running off to help someone else.

She started the van and sat there while it warmed up. Her van was getting up there in age and liked the cold winter months less and less. She tucked the jewelry into the console between the seats. It was starting to snow. Sage wanted to go check on the progress of Cliff's Christmas gift before heading home.

"Maybe I'll head home and call instead," she said, thinking out loud and putting the van in gear. "Cliff should be there at any time, and I haven't even started supper yet."

She pulled into the driveway and Cliff pulled in right behind her. She opened the rear doors of the van and waited for her boyfriend to help her with her tree.

"This is getting to be a thing," he said, joking with her. "Come for supper and get put to work."

"If you open your tree farm you'll have to get used to towing the trees around," Sage replied. "Look at this as practice for when that time comes."

"Why are there two trees, and in pots?"

"The bigger tree is going in my living room. After Christmas I intend to plant it outside at the end of the driveway. The other tree I was hoping you could drop off at Gabby's salon on your way home and set it next to the front door as a surprise for her."

"I can do that. Let me put it in the back of my truck right now so I don't forget," Cliff replied. "And then we'll get yours in the house if you hold the cats, so they don't get out."

They cats were afraid of the tree and instead of running toward the open door they ran for the upstairs. Sage took advantage of the situation and returned to the van to bring in her new decorations and presents she had bought earlier.

Cliff set the tree in front of the bay window where Sage had cleared a space to place it. The cats slowly returned to the living room and approached the tree cautiously. Cliff twirled the tree to put the fullest part facing forward. When it moved, the cats ran again.

"Too bad they won't react like that once the lights and other decorations are on it. They already pulled the lights down out of the window," Sage said. "Maybe I can set the gifts out far enough around it, so they won't be able to get to the tree."

"Good luck with that," Cliff said, laughing.

"I did get plastic ornaments today they can't break," she replied, holding up a box.

"Smart. You may have to use them for a few years until they get older."

"That's okay. Sometimes it's good to change things up," she said, piling the new decorations on the bay window next to the tree.

"So, what's for supper?" Cliff asked.

"Meatball subs. I have to heat up the meatballs and toast the rolls and then we can eat."

They moved to the kitchen and left the cats to investigate the tree.

"Did you find a gift for your parents yet?" Sage asked, setting the pot with the meatballs and sauce on the stove.

"No, and I'm running out of time. They're not materialistic people, which makes it even harder. My mom does collect first edition books, but those show up few and far between. My dad doesn't collect anything."

"Did you check online for any first edition books?" Sage asked, stirring the meatballs, and turning on the oven.

"She doesn't collect just any book because they are first editions. She knows what books she likes and searches for those."

"That makes it more difficult," Sage replied. "Want a beer?"

"Please. Did you find something for your mom?"

"I did, and for Gabby. Let me show you."

Sage showed him the gifts and like a typical man, he responded by saying they were nice. Cliff didn't seem interested in jewelry and she was glad she hadn't bought him anything at *All That Glitters.*

"Did you get anything for your dad and his wife?" Cliff asked.

"I did. This year I bought him a new coin for his collection, and I got his wife a new teapot for her collection. I usually give him something I've made, but I decided to change things up this year. They're already wrapped and in the back den. He said he would stop by Christmas Day on the way to see her family for dinner."

"That's nice, at least you'll get to see him," Cliff replied. "Wait until you see what Rory got for Gabby."

"Tell me," Sage said, spreading mozzarella cheese on the subs and popping them in the oven so the cheese would melt.

"You have to swear to keep it a secret. Do you remember last summer when Gabby was looking at the jacuzzies when we went to the home show in Boston?"

"He didn't?"

"He did. He got her the dark blue one with the silver sparkles she liked. It's going to be delivered four days after Christmas. He needs to build a platform on the back of her house, and he can't do it before because she'll know something is up. He took a picture of the tub at the show, and he folded up the picture and put it in a ring box. She'll think she's getting jewelry and will be so shocked when she unfolds the paper inside."

"I hope he's going to let her open it over here on Christmas Eve so we can all see her reaction."

"He said he was going to give it to her during the gift exchange here."

"That is so awesome. I know where a few of our cookouts will be from now on," Sage said, pulling the cookie sheet from the oven. "And I'm sure after they're married, and Rory moves in he'll use it after a long day at work."

"More than likely," Cliff agreed, watching Sage place the subs on the table. "Those look awesome. I'm getting another beer. You need one?"

"I'm good," she replied, sitting down. "Let's eat so we can decorate my tree."

Despite Sage missing her usual ornaments the tree came out beautifully done in the blues and purples she chose. The cats batted at a few of the ornaments as they were added to the lower branches, but Sage spoke firmly to them, and they finally gave up, lying on the tree skirt under the tree watching from there.

Sage brought out the few gifts she had wrapped and set them under the tree. She stepped back and smiled.

"Looks almost as beautiful as you," Cliff said, wrapping his arms around her waist from behind. "No star?"

"Thank you, sir. It's pretty spectacular for using only plastic ornaments. I looked all over the attic and couldn't find my star for the top of the tree. I don't remember what I did with it last year when I packed everything away."

"It's okay. The tree is nice without a topper," he replied.

"What are you wearing tomorrow night to the open house?" Sage asked.

"I'm wearing my black dress slacks and my red Christmas sweater."

"Please tell me it's not an ugly sweater?"

"No, it's a nice dress sweater. I wouldn't embarrass you or my parents by wearing an ugly sweater there. But I do have a crazy one for the Christmas Eve party here."

"That I can live with seeing as it is an ugly sweater party here. I'm wearing my red velour calf-length dress with white fur trim. We'll be the best-looking couple there."

"And now, I need to get home. I have a lot to do tomorrow before the open house. I'll see you at eight," he said, giving her a quick kiss.

"I'll see you then," she said, closing the door behind him.

As soon as his truck left the driveway she turned off the outside Christmas lights and unplugged the tree lights. The cats followed her up the stairs and made themselves comfortable on her bed. Sage crawled in next to them and the family fell asleep.

Nine o'clock the next morning, Ralph was there to pick up the room dividers for his wife. He was so pleased with the finished product; he not only paid her for her work but gave her a Christmas bonus as well. She locked up her shop and headed for town to pick up Cliff's gift.

She parked in the rear parking lot of *Signs* so her van wouldn't be seen from Main Street. Owner Barry Stump was ringing up another customer and signaled he would be right with her. She walked around the shop admiring the workmanship of the sign maker.

"Sage, did you bring your van?" Barry asked.

"I did. Is it ready to go?"

"It is. Would you like to see it?" he asked, leading her to the back room. "What do you think?"

"It's wonderful. Cliff is going to love it. You haven't said anything to anyone have you? The tree farm is a secret the Fulton's want to keep quiet for now."

"I didn't breathe a word to anyone," he replied. "Personally, I think it's a great idea. I just hope I'm still around to buy one of the first trees off their farm."

"You will be," Sage assured him. "I brought some padding to wrap it in to get it home. I'll go get it while you run my charge card."

They worked together to wrap the sign and move it out to the van. Sage thanked him and got in her vehicle to leave.

"What else do I need to do today besides food shopping for the party and Christmas day dinner?" she pondered out loud while reading the messages on her phone.

Gabby left a message stating she and Rory would be about fifteen minutes late tonight getting to the house. Her mom left a message asking what she could bring for dinner on Christmas day. She messaged her back and told her to bring some kind of vegetables.

Sage had ordered the prime rib in advance from the grocery store so it would be ready when she got there. The grocery store was busy as all get out as no one wanted to be shopping at the last minute. The store closed at noon on Christmas Eve day for the family to enjoy the holiday and wouldn't reopen until the day after Christmas. She grabbed a cart and headed for the meat department to pick up her order.

"Merry Christmas, Sage! How is your mom?" Sam, the butcher, asked.

"She's good, thank you. How is your family?"

"They're all excited about Santa's visit," he replied, smiling.

"How old are your kids now?"

"Three, five, and eight."

"You have your hands full," Sage said. "Is my order all ready?"

"It is. You must be feeding an army with what you ordered."

"Cliff can put away food like a whole army himself and so can Rory," she replied, laughing, and reaching for her package. "But to be fair, I do have quite a few people just drop in, so I have to have extra on hand."

"Are you going to the Flemming's open house tonight?" Sage asked.

"No, not with three small children and Santa's visit to prepare for. My wife and I went last year, and it was a lot of fun. At least until her sons started acting up and disrupted the party."

"That seems to happen a lot," Sage mumbled.

"Have a good time tonight and have a great holiday," he said, turning to wait on another customer.

For the next hour Sage wandered up and down the aisles filling her cart with finger foods and other necessities for her Christmas Eve party and dinner the following day. She wanted everything to be perfect as not only was Cliff going to be there for the first time, but his parents would be as well. She also needed snacks to eat throughout the day as people stopped by to visit.

When she arrived home, she closed the door between the mud room and the kitchen so the cats couldn't get out and unloaded all the groceries. The cats were in heaven as every time Sage emptied a paper bag, she tossed it on the floor for the cats. They ran in and out of the bags and jumped on top of them where the other one was hiding and waiting to attack.

Sage finished putting the groceries away and left the cats playing with the bags while she went to the dining room to wrap some gifts. The gifts were all wrapped and placed around the tree. Sage went out to the van to bring in Cliff's sign. It was big and heavy, and she had to make several stops between the van and her mud room. She finally made it to the living room and slid the huge present behind the tree up against the wall under the bay window.

Back in the kitchen all was quiet. Smokey and Motorboat had worn themselves out and were asleep together in one of the paper bags. Sage folded the rest of the bags and set them in the laundry room. She still had four hours that she could prep some of the food she would be cooking in the morning.

By seven-thirty she had showered, put on light make-up and styled her hair. The fur-lined dress showed off her slim figure. She finished her ensemble with perfectly matched red velour flats and silver snowflake earrings. Happy with the way she looked, she was sure her boyfriend would be proud to walk into the open house with her on his arm.

Cliff walked through the door and let out a long whistle. Sage twirled, the dress encircling her.

"Don't you look handsome in your Christmas red," she said, returning his hug.

"You look stunning," he said, kissing her. "I didn't see Gabby's car out there. Are they running late?"

"She messaged me earlier and said they would be about fifteen minutes late," Sage replied. "I was so busy I forgot to turn on the outdoor lights. Gabby would be upset if she arrives, and they're not on to greet her."

"I borrowed my mom's SUV for us to ride in to go to the open house. She and dad are taking his car."

"Gabby had said we could take her car, but your mom's is so much roomier," Sage replied, chasing the cats down off the kitchen table. "I often wonder what trouble these two get into when I'm not home."

"How have they been with the tree?"

"So far, so good. It's still standing, which is a good thing, I guess. I find ornaments scattered around the floor and put them back on the tree."

"Gotta love them," Cliff said, scratching behind Motorboat's ears.

"We're here," Gabby yelled, coming through the door.

"Everyone looks so nice. We need some pictures," Sage said, picking up her cell phone.

Gabby was dressed in a bright green dress while Rory was in a three-piece suit with a light up green Christmas tie.

"Dude, you trying to show me up?" Cliff asked.

"No, these are the only dress clothes I own," he replied. "Gabby said I couldn't wear jeans and that's just about all I own."

"I'll drive," Cliff stated. "Are we ready to go?"

"It's starting to snow," Gabby said. "A little bit of Christmas magic for a magical night."

CHAPTER THREE

The long driveway leading up to the Flemming mansion was lined in brightly lit candy canes. There wasn't an inch on the house not covered in Christmas lights. At the front door was a valet podium manned with four valets.

Cliff pulled up in line and waited his turn. Gabby was going on about the lights and how she wanted her house to look like this one sometime in the future. Sage was more interested in a woman who was peering in one of the rear windows at the back of the porch.

"Doesn't that look like Mrs. Ripple?"

"It is her. What is she doing?" Rory replied.

"The question is, where is her husband? She can't be here by herself," Sage said.

"He must be inside, and she wandered off. Someone needs to tell him she's out here," Sage said. "Why is she backing up? She's going to fall off the porch if she doesn't stop."

Cliff pulled the car up to the podium and they all got out. He was handed a ticket, and they went up the stairs.

"I want to check on Mrs. Ripple before we go inside," Sage stated.

They heard a faint help me coming from the back of the porch and took off running. Mrs. Ripple had fallen off the porch and had landed in the bushes down below. Her hair was tangled in the branches, and she was fighting to free herself.

Cliff and Rory jumped down off the porch to help her. Mr. Ripple had discovered his wife was missing and had come outside to find her. Between the three men, they managed to release her from the bushes and get her back up on the porch.

"Cora, what were you doing out here?" her husband asked her.

"I was hot."

"Thank you for helping my wife," George said to the guys. "Come on, Cora, it's time to go home."

"He wanted the marshmallows," Cora mumbled. "Why didn't he just ask for them?"

"Come on, honey. I'll make you some hot chocolate at home and put marshmallows in it," George said, coaxing his wife to the front stairs. "She has a thing for marshmallows."

"I'm sorry you have to leave," Gabby said.

"It's okay. I need to spend as much time as I can with my wife because after the new year she'll be going into memory care in Moosehead. I was trying to make our last holiday together one she would remember but her memory goes in and out."

"He wanted the marshmallows," Cora insisted.

"Who wanted the marshmallows?" Sage asked. "I saw you looking in the window."

Cora stared blankly at Sage.

"I don't know what you're talking about. Come on, George, let's go into the party," she said, taking her husband's hand.

"Okay but just for a little while," he said, shaking his head. "Thank you, again."

The group watched the couple walk away.

"Poor Mr. Ripple," Gabby said, sadly.

"Shall we go inside?" Cliff asked. "I'm starving and the food is supposed to be incredible here."

They were stopped at the door, and each was given a raffle ticket. They dropped their canned goods into the box next to the entry table. The place was gorgeous as more decorations had been added since the two women were there at the beginning of the week. The double split staircase was now lined with lit garland on the banisters and alternating red and gold poinsettias on each stair. A decorated tree that had to be at least twenty feet high was in the center of the split staircases. Under it were piles of gifts, all sizes and shapes which were to be used for the raffle winners.

If your number was pulled you could go to the tree and choose a gift. They had timed it just right and a number was called minutes after they entered the door. Sheriff White stepped forward with the winning number. He picked his gift and walked to the entry way to open it passing by Sage and the group.

"Sheriff White, Merry Christmas!" Sage said, hugging him around the gift he was holding. "I'm so glad you came."

"I wasn't going to, but your mother talked me into it. And now, I have won a prize."

"Are you going to open it now?" Gabby asked.

"Right now," he said, tearing at the festive wrapping paper.

A fully loaded tackle box with all the latest and fanciest lures, weights, and multiple size hooks was unveiled. The gift fit the sheriff as he loved to fish at the lake on his days off during the summer and he also competed in several fishing competitions. He had no idea what was in the gift, but by chance he had picked the best thing he could have gotten for himself.

"That's awesome," Rory said, checking out the lures, being a fisherman himself. "You better lock that up in your car or it might disappear."

"You kids have never been here before. You take your gift to the coat closet, and they tag it with your name and the last three numbers of your ticket. That way, you can enjoy the party without carrying things around or having to walk all the way out to your car."

"How are you doing?" Sage asked him, knowing this was his first Christmas without Ella, his wife.

"I'm good. I'm still adjusting to living by myself, but your mom doesn't let me sit home and dwell in silence. Sarah has been wonderful since Ella passed. She's around here somewhere but she's such a social butterfly she doesn't stay still very long," the sheriff replied.

"I'm going to hit the buffet. Anyone want to join me?" Cliff asked.

"I'm in," Rory and Gabby replied at the same time.

"Me, too," the sheriff said.

"I'm going to find my mom and then I'll join you to eat," Sage said.

As she walked around looking for her mom, Mrs. Flemming approached her dressed in a floor-length green velour gown which swirled around her when she walked. She had on a sparkling red and green tiara making her look like she was royalty. She was smiling, no she was beaming, at how well the open house was going.

"Sage, people love the cabinet. I haven't opened it yet for my husband or my guests to see the interior gun case you created. He was called away to take an overseas phone call but promised he'd make it back as quickly as he could so I can present him with his gift. Meanwhile, enjoy yourself and it's time to call a new number. Excuse me," she said, hurrying off.

"Sage, you look wonderful," her mom said, coming up behind her. "Where's Cliff? He did come with you, didn't he?"

"He's here. He, Rory, and the sheriff are diving into the buffet."

"I should have known. Doesn't Gerald look great? He didn't want to come tonight, but I talked him into it. And I hope you don't mind but I invited him over for Christmas Eve and for Christmas dinner. I don't want him being at home alone."

"Of course, I don't mind. I'm glad he's coming to join us. How does it feel to have three days off in a row from work?"

"I'll be so busy it will go by in a blink."

"Were all the gifts picked up this morning from the library?"

"Every last one of them. We had several parents crying as they loaded their cars, because they couldn't believe the gifts they received for their kids. I called the food pantry to see if they had any extra dinner packages and they did so I sent several single moms who were new to the area over to get Christmas dinner. They were all so appreciative."

"It's time to call another number," Mrs. Flemming yelled from the staircase. "234899."

"That's mine," Sage exclaimed. "I won a raffle."

She handed her ticket to the hostess and looked over the gifts. Smaller gifts had been placed on the tree branches. Sage knew Mrs. Flemming had shopped at *All That Glitters* so she took one of the smaller gifts off the tree.

"Open it up. Let's see what you got," her mom said.

"Let's walk to the dining room so I can open it in front of everyone," Sage suggested.

The group was sitting in the corner, eating, drinking, and laughing. Sage and her mom walked up to the table and Merry Christmas' were exchanged.

"Sage won a raffle," her mom announced.

She held out her hand with the package in it.

"You picked a small one," Gabby said, disappointed with her friend's pick. "Open it."

Sage removed the paper to find a blue velour box with *All That Glitters* stamped on the top of it. She flipped open the lid to find a woman's gold dress watch with twelve diamonds set into the watch face instead of numbers.

"Let us see. What did you get?" Gabby asked.

She held up the open box so people could see the gift inside.

"Nice," Cliff said and went back to eating.

I can tell I'll never get a bit of jewelry from him.

Sage and her mom filled plates and joined the rest of the group to eat. More raffle numbers were called but none belonged to anyone in the group. They finished eating and were cleaning up their table when the next number called belonged to Rory.

He grabbed a medium sized gift and tore open the paper. It was a flat screen television which Gabby claimed for use in her salon. Rory rolled his eyes and went to check in the gift at the coat closet.

Many guests had come to Sage to tell her how much they loved the cabinet she restored for Mrs. Flemming and asked for her business card. In the first hour they were there she had given out over twenty cards with promises to call her after the new year.

"I never imagined the cabinet would be so great for business. And no one has even seen the inside yet," Sage said to Gabby, handing out another card.

The friends socialized with the other locals and were thoroughly enjoying themselves. Cliff had won a hundred-dollar gift certificate to the *Cupston Hardware Store* and Gabby had won a gold butterfly necklace set with multiple-colored stones set in the wings. She had taken advice from Sage and chose a smaller gift which also turned out to be from *All That Glitters*. The only one not to win anything yet was Sage's mom.

Mrs. Flemming announced her husband still hadn't come out of his den, but she wanted people to see the inside of the Victorian cabinet and the incredible work Sage had done on the gift. She walked into the parlor with the guests following behind. The outside of the cabinet had been visible all night and people were curious about what was inside.

"This is the real reason for the cabinet," she announced, reaching for the door to show her guests what Sage had created. "It's a new gun cabinet."

She opened the door a few inches and a hand fell out. People screamed and ran from the room. Mrs. Flemming flung the cabinet door open to find her husband stuffed in the bottom of it, dead.

"Phillip!" Marion Flemming yelled. "Get him out of there!"

"No, leave him where he is," the sheriff said from the back of the room. "Don't touch him."

Sheriff White ran forward and yelled for the room to be cleared.

"No one leaves the house," he ordered.

Sage stood at the parlor door watching the sheriff. Deputy Bell was also at the party and went out to man the front door. A call was placed to the M.E. to come to the Flemming mansion. Sheriff White escorted Mrs. Flemming out of the room and into a private area off the kitchen.

"What's going on?" Stephen, the younger son asked, entering the kitchen from a set of back stairs. "Mom, what's wrong?"

"Stephen, where have you been tonight?" the sheriff asked.

"I've been up in my room. I don't do parties and crowds."

"You've been up there since when?"

"I don't know. I came down to get something to eat before the party started and took it back upstairs. Why? What's it to you?"

"Stephen, stop being so rude to the sheriff," his mother said, angrily. "I don't know who you think you are talking to people like that."

He glared at his mother not liking the fact she had corrected him in front of others.

"Your father is dead," his mother blurted out.

"Seriously?" Stephen asked flippantly. "Father is dead. Ya, right."

"Your father IS dead," the sheriff stated.

"Did you see anyone in the kitchen or parlor prior to the open house starting?" the sheriff asked.

"I saw lots of people. The caterers, the wait staff, the maids, and Roger our butler. There were people everywhere. Truthfully, I wasn't paying much attention to anything but my plate."

"Stephen, really? I should have stepped in to raise my sons long ago, but I didn't, and this is the result; rude and arrogant," Mrs. Flemming muttered. "Sheriff White, I apologize for his rudeness."

"Can I go back upstairs now?" Stephen asked, shifting his weight nervously. "Crowds make me nervous."

"Do you even care your father is gone?" his mother asked.

"I care, but I'm not going to break down and make a fool of myself in front of all these people like you are. Can I go now?"

"Go to your room and stay there," his mother ordered.

Stephen opened his mouth to say something but changed his mind. He glared at his mother and the sheriff as he left the kitchen. Sage and Cliff had been watching from the door. Deputy Bell came into the kitchen and had a quiet conversation with the sheriff. He shook his head yes to whatever Bell was saying to him and the deputy returned to the front door.

"I wonder what that was about?" Sage whispered to Cliff.

"I don't know but I'd be looking at Stephen for this. He's a real jerk and I wouldn't put it past him to do something like this."

"You know Stephen?"

"I sure do. We went to school together. He was a jerk back then and it seems he has gotten worse since then."

"Why was he a jerk?" Sage asked.

"He was always getting into trouble and his dad would bail him out every time. He threw money around to get what he wanted and had no respect for any of the teachers or the principal. If he got into bad trouble his dad would make a sizeable donation to the school for a needed project and all was swept under the carpet," Cliff replied. "He had few friends and the ones he did have were all bought and paid for."

"Maybe that's why he spends so much time playing video games. He has no social life," Sage surmised.

"Neither Phillip nor Stephen had any kind of social life. They looked to each other for company and pretty much isolated themselves from everyone else."

"Still, it makes no sense he would kill his father. He depended on him for money and self-preservation," Sage stated. "Although I did see a side of the brothers that was pretty violent when they were fighting over the video game at the five and dime. Their tempers were out of control."

"Phillip could be a bully when he wanted to be, too. He beat up many a kid in high school and Daddy always came through to smooth things over with the parents or anyone else who was considering pressing charges against him. Phillip wasn't well liked then and still isn't now," Cliff said. "He was thrown off his bowling team because of his bad temper just this past summer."

"Did you like him?" Sage asked her boyfriend.

"Nope, not in the least," he replied. "Phillip Jr. has a lot of enemies, women included. He's always been a womanizer."

"And with half the town going in and out of here tonight it could have been anyone who killed Mr. Flemming," Sage replied. "Here comes the sheriff."

"Best estimate the M.E. can give us right now is Phillip was killed between four and six o'clock. He was hit on the back of the head with a blunt object."

"Mrs. Flemming said he went to take a call around four-thirty so that cuts the window down even more for the murder to have taken place," Sage said. "Cliff was just telling me some interesting things about Phillip Jr. and Stephen. You might want to talk to him a little later."

"I will. Deputy Bell and I agreed we can't keep the whole town locked up here at the mansion while we do our investigation. And because of the time frame from the M.E., it seems Phillip was killed before the open house even started. We're taking names and letting people go home. It's such a shame really. This has always been a town highlight of the Christmas season."

"Sage, I'm going into the parlor to see if we can determine what the blunt object might have been that was used in the murder. If you promise not to touch anything you can come and look around. You have good instincts when it comes to things like this."

"My fingerprints are already all over the cabinet and around the room. We did deliver the cabinet at the beginning of the week to Mrs. Flemming," Sage said.

"We?'

"Yes, Gabby and I were in the room when her sons moved the cabinet from my van into the parlor."

"So, their prints are already on the cabinet as well as yours. I'll make a note of that as the cabinet door and handles will be dusted for prints," the sheriff said, taking a small notebook out of his shirt pocket. "Cliff, you are welcome to join us in the parlor."

"I'm going to see if Gabby and Rory want a ride back to Sage's house to pick up their vehicle. They might not want to hang around here any longer."

"Tell Gabby I'll call her in the morning," Sage said as Cliff walked away promising he'd be back shortly to bring her home.

They walked from the kitchen to the parlor. The Christmas tree was still loaded with raffle gifts underneath as the party had been cut short by several hours. People were still milling about but it was mostly workers and mansion staff who had remained to clean up after the party concluded. The atmosphere had gone from festive and happy to quiet and sad.

Deputy Durst had been called in to work and was dusting the cabinet for prints. Bell had finished taking names and was perusing the parlor area for any clues to help in the investigation. Sage walked around, her hands at her side.

The back of the cabinet caught her attention. Standing there she could see the windows which ran along the side of the room where Cora Ripple had been looking in from the porch.

I wonder if Cora saw something.

"Mrs. Flemming said her husband went into his den around four-thirty to take a call. She never disturbed him when he was on a business call, so she doesn't know when the call was concluded," Sheriff White stated. "And she didn't think about it as she had last minute things to check on for the party and guests started to arrive at six o'clock."

Cora couldn't have seen who did it through the window. It was well after the time frame the M.E. set for time of death. Unless the murderer returned to the scene for some reason.

"Sheriff, one of the bronze statues is missing from the corner table," Deputy Bell said. "It is a set of angels, and it looks like the middle one is missing. There's a dust free ring where something sat."

"Bell, go get Mrs. Flemming so we can verify if the statue was there in the first place and if it was, exactly what was it?" the sheriff requested.

Mrs. Flemming walked to the table and verified there had been three statues there last she knew. The missing angel was a guardian angel who had her wings wrapped around a small child. The sheriff thanked her and told her she could return to the kitchen.

"Unfortunately, because of the size of the statue it could have been dropped into a purse or hidden underneath a coat," Sheriff White said.

"Or, it could have been buried inside a pot of a plant in the room," Sage said, pointing to a large Elephant Ear plant in the back corner of the room. "The tip of the wing is sticking out of the dirt."

The sheriff put on a pair of gloves and carefully pushed the dirt aside which was surrounding the hidden angel. Once he pulled it out the group could see blood on the statue.

"This is definitely the murder weapon," the sheriff said, depositing the statue in an evidence bag, sealing it, and initialing the front of the bag.

"The statue was in the room already, so it doesn't look like the murder was premeditated. It looks to be more like a murder of opportunity instead," Bell stated.

"I'm going out and walk around the buffet area and listen to the staff," Sage said. "They may know something but are afraid to say anything which could jeopardize their job."

The catering service was already breaking down the buffet area. They were packing the food in plastic containers and filling cardboard boxes with the containers to send to the local homeless shelter and woman's shelter in Cupston. Sage poked around what food was still on the table. She grabbing a plate and filled it with deviled eggs and other finger foods before it was taken away so she wouldn't look so suspicious milling about.

"If you ask me, he got what was coming to him," one of the waitresses mumbled to another waitress. "I said I would never come back here to work again after what he did to my sister, but Mrs. Flemming pays so well I couldn't resist the job. I can do all my Christmas shopping using this one paycheck."

"I'm surprised she let you back in the house after your sister's lawsuit against her husband."

"Mrs. Flemming isn't the kind of person who holds a grudge. Besides, she admitted what Phillip had done was wrong and sided with Emily in the lawsuit. Her husband was the one who had a fierce temper and held grudges."

"You can clearly see who Phillip and Stephen take after."

They moved away from Sage when they discovered she was listening to their conversation. She boldly walked up to the two waitresses and asked about the lawsuit.

"It was all over town even though Mr. Flemming tried to silence everyone. I can't believe you didn't hear about it. Phillip, the son, strung my sister along making her think they were going to be married until he got what he wanted and then he dumped her cold. She turned up pregnant and sued him for child support, but Mr. Flemming gave her a lump sum settlement to drop the suit and leave Cupston. In return she agreed not to use the last name of Flemming for her son and signed a gag order to never discuss the settlement with anyone."

"How long ago was that?" Sage asked.

"Let's see, Anthony is six, so it was a while ago. Emily moved away before he was born, and it broke my dad's heart. She's happy now where she is and so is her son."

"Emily's not the only one either. I believe Phillip Jr. and Stephen have three kids between them," the second waitress replied. "Between you and me, I don't know how Mrs. Flemming put up with everything she did all these years. Her husband, not to speak ill of the dead, was no angel either when it came to affairs."

"Thank you for talking to me. I'll pass on what you said to the sheriff as it appears many more people have a motive to want Mr. Flemming dead," Sage said, taking her plate and heading back to the parlor.

"There are many people who will be happy he is gone," the butler whispered to her as he walked past her and into the kitchen.

That was strange.

The M.E. was in the process of strapping the body to the gurney as Sage returned to the parlor. He and the sheriff were deep in conversation, so Sage stood quietly at the door waiting for them to finish. The body was removed from the house as Mrs. Flemming stood at the bottom of the stairs flanked on either side of her by her sons. It was the first time Sage had seen Phillip Jr. that night.

"We need to search your sons' bedrooms," the sheriff told Mrs. Flemming. "Do you give your consent?"

"Not without a search warrant, you don't," Phillip Jr., stated in protest. "I did learn some things from my father and if you don't have a warrant you don't get past the bottom of the stairs."

"Last I knew this was still my house and not yours," his mother replied. "Sheriff, you search wherever you need to if it will help in the investigation."

"Thank you. If you please, keep your sons down here while we complete the search. And Phillip, we still need to question you as to your whereabouts earlier this evening."

"Roger, please take the sheriff to Phillip's and Stephen's rooms."

"Yes, Ma'am. Should I stay while they search, or can I return to my duties?" the butler asked.

"I know you have things to do, so yes, you can return to doing what has to be done," Mrs. Flemming said. "Boys, to the kitchen, now!"

Sage told the sheriff all the things she found out talking to the waitresses, and the butler's strange comment to her as he passed her to go into the kitchen.

"This is even stranger," the sheriff replied. "When the M.E. removed the body from the cabinet they found a red sticky substance on Mr. Flemming's suitcoat where the body would have been held to pick him up. And there were traces of the same substance on the statue."

"I don't think that's so strange," Sage replied, telling him about the incident with Cora Ripple outside on the porch.

"She said they were fighting over marshmallows?"

"She did, but when I questioned her about it she blanked out and couldn't remember anything about what she had just said."

"Her mind is fading fast, and she might not have seen anything at all, you don't know," the sheriff said. "I have a search to complete and I think I saw Cliff pull in just now. Your mom invited me over to your house for the holidays. I hope that's okay?"

"It's fine. We're glad you're going to join us. I'm going in to thank Mrs. Flemming and offer to take back the cabinet. I'm sure after what's happened she doesn't want it in her house," Sage stated. "I can always stick it in my storage trailer and maybe sell it a year or two down the road when this incident is only a distant memory."

"I got a look at what you did inside to create a gun case. If we can figure out a way to put a more secured lock on it I may buy it for my house if she doesn't want to keep it. I deal with dead bodies in my work, so it doesn't bother me that Mr. Flemming was found in the cabinet."

"I'll keep that in mind," Sage replied.

"Good, Plummer is here with his camera so we can start the search upstairs. I guess I'll see you tomorrow night," the sheriff said, walking away.

Sage walked into the kitchen. Mrs. Flemming was sitting with her butler quietly conversing in the corner. Phillip and Stephen were in the opposite corner eating heartily as if nothing had happened tonight. As Sage walked by the brothers she noticed Phillip's hands. There was dirt under the fingernails. The same dark dirt which was in the pot in the parlor.

She pulled out her phone and texted the sheriff of her suspicions and then walked over to Mrs. Flemming. Roger, the butler, was holding her hand and comforting her.

"Oh, Sage, you're still here," she said, pulling her hand away from Roger's hand. "I'm glad. I have something to ask you."

"I came to see if you wanted me to remove the cabinet from the house. Under the circumstances, I can buy it back and you won't have to see it again," Sage said.

"I would like it removed but you don't have to buy it back. After Christmas you can come retrieve the cabinet and the boys will help you load it in your van."

"I couldn't just take it back," Sage started to protest.

"You did the work I requested, and I appreciate it. I do not have any use for a gun cabinet now as I will be selling my husband's guns. I don't like them, and I only tolerated them being in the house because my Phillip loved them so. Please take the cabinet back and see if you can find someone who loves guns as much as my husband did and sell it to them."

"Did you ever think to stop and ask us if we'd like to have father's guns?" Phillip asked, through a full mouth.

"I don't have to ask you anything. You two are the last people who should have guns at their disposal. Things are going to change around here, and you're not going to like it. The guns will be removed from the house," their mother said. "I don't want to end up the same way your father did, dead."

"I suppose he told you to say that," Stephen asked, glaring at the butler.

"You leave Roger out of this. Your father babied you and never once held you responsible for a single thing in your life. The free-flowing money is going to stop, and you will be getting jobs, both of you."

"What's the matter, Roger? You don't want us spending OUR family's money so you and my mother will have more when you get married?

"That's enough, Stephen," his mother warned.

"We know about you and Roger and have known for a long time. And father did, too. How do we know it wasn't one of you who killed him so you could be together?" Stephen replied, throwing his mother under the bus.

The sheriff had come into the kitchen and was listening intently. He stepped forward and walked directly to Phillip and asked to see his hands. Phillip refused and tucked them under his legs.

"Get a warrant," he snarled.

"I don't need one. The murder weapon was buried inside a potted plant in the parlor, and you have dirt under your fingernails which I'm sure didn't get there by playing video games. Bell, cuff him and take him in for questioning."

"I'll call dad's attorney for you," Stephen said, rushing from the room.

Phillip had to be helped up as he refused to stand to be cuffed. Bell forced his hands out in front of him so they could be photographed before he left the premises. The cuffs were placed on him, and he was dragged out of the house kicking and screaming like a small child who hadn't got their way in a toy store.

"Do you really think Phillip killed his father?" Mrs. Flemming asked, the tears starting to flow again.

"I don't know, Marion, but it doesn't look good because of the dirt under his fingernails," the sheriff answered. "We're done upstairs. You can send your attorney to the station to be present for Phillip's questioning. You and Stephen will have to come down to the station for an interview. As long as you promise me everyone in your family will stay put and not leave Cupston, you can come down the day after Christmas. We have all the evidence we need from the house."

"Will Phillip be able to come home for Christmas?" she asked.

"I can't promise that right now. It depends on his interview," the sheriff said, honestly. "I also need the members of your permanent staff to come to the station and give a statement. The M.E. stated be believes the death occurred between four and six which would have been before any of your guests arrived."

"But my husband went into the den at four-thirty to take his call."

"That cuts the time frame down even more," the sheriff replied. "We searched his den and saw no evidence of a struggle in there or blood. For some reason he went to the parlor to more than likely meet someone there and that's where the murder took place. We noticed a rear door out of the den leads to the hallway between the kitchen and the parlor."

"Yes, my husband could have traveled from his den to the parlor without anyone seeing him doing it," Marion replied. "So, you're telling me someone in my household probably killed my husband?"

"The investigation is still under way. I can't answer that question at the present moment."

"I'm not waiting until the day after Christmas. My son and myself, along with my staff will be at the station first thing in the morning, Christmas Eve day or not. I need to know who it was who did this," Mrs. Flemming said. "I'm not sleeping in my own home with a murderer."

"Very well, I will expect you at nine. Marion, I am so sorry this happened. Good night," he said. "Let's go guys. We have an interview to conduct and evidence to look over."

"Cliff is back to get me so I will be leaving, too," Sage said. "You said you had something to ask me?"

"I do. I know you and your mother work at the family gift project every year. I also know you have a good-sized attic at your house. Don't look surprised. Your mom told me they store all the wrapping supplies at your house for the next year. Will it be possible for you to bring your van the day after Christmas, pick up the cabinet and empty the gifts from around the raffle tree and store them in your attic? I would love them to be used for your families who need help next year."

"That would be wonderful, but are you sure you can't use the gifts for your family?" Sage asked.

"My sons have all they need. Their gifts are already under the tree in our private living area. Please, take the gifts and put them to good use."

"I will, I promise. LouAnn will be so excited to have such a great head start for next year. We are always short on gifts for adults and this generous offer will help immensely. Thank you."

"If you don't mind, we weren't able to raise what we normally do for the food pantry because the open house was cut short. I would like to take all of the money from the raffle ticket sales and donate it to the food pantry along with what food we did collect instead of splitting the money fifty-fifty with your charity. I think the gifts will more than make up for your half of the money."

"I'm sure that will be fine with LouAnn. I'm leaving now and I'm very sorry about your husband. I will be here the day after Christmas," Sage said.

"Merry Christmas, Sage," Mrs. Flemming said, sighing deeply.

"Are you okay?" Cliff asked his girlfriend as they walked from the kitchen.

"I am. It's just that I never pegged Phillip as being so stupid that he would leave dirt under his fingernails if he buried the murder weapon. He may have a temper and be a miserable excuse for a human being, but I can't see him being so careless."

"Hopefully the answers will come out in his interrogation."

"I don't know, he was pretty adamant about having a search warrant about everything. It doesn't seem like he will cooperate in any kind of questioning," Sage replied, stopping in front of the tree at the bottom of the stairs.

"There's got to be at least seventy-five gifts left over if not closer to a hundred. I guess it's a good thing someone will benefit from them."

Sage had a funny feeling she was being watched. She looked up to the top of the stairs and Stephen was standing there glaring at her with such intense hatred it made her shiver.

"Get out of my house," he ordered through gritted teeth. "And don't think you'll be getting your hands on any of those gifts no matter what my mother says."

"From what your mother says, you have no say in this house, and she wants these gifts to go to the less fortunate," Sage replied. "Not you."

Stephen flew into a rage and came flying down the stairs after Sage.

CHAPTER FOUR

Cliff dashed in front of Sage just as Stephen hit the bottom stair. Stephen raised his fist to hit Sage, and Cliff tackled him to the ground and pinned him so he couldn't move. Her son's screaming brought his mother and the butler running out from the kitchen.

"Cliff, what are you doing to my son?" she asked. "Why do you have him pinned on the floor?"

"Because your son informed my girlfriend she would never get her hands on any of the gifts under the tree, and she disagreed with him, repeating what you said in the kitchen. He flew down the stairs and was going to punch Sage in the face, so I tackled him and stopped him from doing it," Cliff replied, struggling to hold Stephen still.

"Sage, is this true?" Mrs. Flemming asked.

"It is. I told him you wanted the gifts to go to the less fortunate, and he went ballistic, flew down the stairs, and tried to attack me."

"This night just gets worse and worse. Are you going to press charges?"

"No. But I would request when I return the day after Christmas to pick everything up that he not be anywhere near me while I am doing it. I don't trust him," Sage replied. "Cliff, you can let him up now that his mother is here."

Stephen scrambled to his feet.

"You'll pay for this," he threatened as he ran up the stairs and out of sight.

"I think that boy needs a stint in the military to straighten him out. His father and I talked about it just the other night. Thank you for not pressing charges. I'll see he apologizes to you."

"That's not necessary. Just keep him away from me, please," Sage stated. "And if you don't mind, Cliff will come with me when I pick up the gifts."

"That's fine."

Sage noticed two housekeepers, each one around twenty-five to thirty years old, standing in the corner watching everything. They were whispering to each other, covering their mouths with their hands so no one could see what they were saying. It seemed funny to Sage that with the job they held they each had long fingernails, one done in red and the other in green.

Maybe they had them done for the party. The waitresses said Mrs. Flemming was easy to work for and paid well.

"We'll see you in a couple of days," Sage said, taking Cliff's hand and heading for the door.

They arrived at Sage's house a little after one. Cliff made sure she was safely inside and left for home. The cats had pulled some of the bows off the gifts that were already under the tree which had in turn ripped the wrapping paper underneath where they had been attached.

"Great, now I have to rewrap gifts tomorrow before the party tomorrow night. Way to make extra work for me," she said to Smokey and Motorboat who were sitting on the couch together, tilting their heads as she spoke to them. "Speaking of gifts, I have to have something for Sheriff White to open during the gift exchange. I'll have to run to the five and dime early in the morning before it closes at noon."

She set all the gifts she had to rewrap on the dining room table, turned out the lights and shooed the cats up the stairs to go to bed. Sage fell asleep running the night's events through her head.

Coffee in hand, Sage was out the door the next morning at seven-thirty. She wanted to be at the five and dime when it opened at eight. She had a lot to do before her guests started to arrive at six that evening.

She walked around the store searching for something for the sheriff. Up until this year she never had to buy gifts for men except for her dad who was happy with anything he got as long as his daughter made it in her shop. This was a whole new and somewhat frustrating experience buying for males in her life.

Sage had just picked up a really cool collapsible fishing pole for the sheriff when her cell rang. It was the sheriff. She grabbed a second pole for Rory and headed for the register while answering the call.

"Hello."

"Sage, I wanted to let you know during our questioning of Phillip we found out he had bought his mother four holly bushes for her yard. She has always wanted them on the property, and he planted them that day to surprise her. That was why he claimed to have dirt under his fingernails. Bell went to check out the story and sure enough, the bushes were right where he said they were at the rear of the house near the gazebo."

"I said to Cliff I thought he was too smart to leave dirt under his nails if he buried the murder weapon," Sage replied.

"The reason I am calling is I heard about your close encounter with Stephen after we left last night. For right now, Phillip has been cleared and we are seriously looking at Stephen and his temper. You need to be careful when you return to the mansion."

"Why has Phillip been cleared?"

"At the time of the death, Phillip was in Cupston Christmas shopping. We have several people who witnessed him in town, and he has receipts for everything he bought. The last one is from a fast-food spot and the time stamp on it is six-thirty-three. The manager remembers him sitting there with a female friend eating."

"That was after the window of the murder. He could have committed the murder and then gone to town," Sage replied.

"All his receipts are time stamped and we put them in chronological order. He left the house at three, stopped at *All That Glitters* as his first stop and bought something for his grandmother at three-thirty-five. Accounting for all the receipts, he wouldn't have had time to get home and back to town again during that time frame. He wasn't at the house when it happened."

"His mother must be happy. She did tell me last night that her and her husband discussed making the boys go into the military which could be another motive if their father agreed with the decision," Sage said. "Are you releasing Phillip?"

"We are. Marion Flemming just walked into the station with Stephen, the butler and five other women I assume are maids at the house. I have to go start interviews if I ever want to get out of here today. I'll see you tonight although I'm not sure what time it will be."

"See you when you get there," she said, hanging up.

Sage paid for her items and left the five and dime. She stopped at the grocery store as she had forgotten eggnog when she was shopping the previous day. Her next and final stop was the *Cupston Liquor Store*.

Her home bar was pretty limited, and she needed to have various kinds of alcohol on hand not knowing what people drank. She loaded her cart with rum, whisky, vodka, several types of beers as well as a variety of wines. She even included a bottle of Irish Cream which she loved to put in her coffee during the cold winter months. What wasn't used over the Christmas get togethers would be used at New Years. She finished off her shopping with various types of sodas, juices, and seltzer waters for mixed drinks.

As she stood in line, her mind ran to the past year and how good life had been to her. Her business was flourishing, she had become the proud owner of a cache of beautiful diamonds, she had great friends, and a wonderful new boyfriend. She didn't mind spending the money she was for the holidays because she was paying her good fortune forward to her friends and family.

Sage was back at home before noon and got busy with the food preparation. She had a big pot of eggs boiling on the stove that would be made into deviled eggs. Sweet and sour meatballs were simmering in one crockpot next to a second one holding lobster mac and cheese. A large tossed green salad was cooling in the fridge.

She had bought Christmas cookies and cupcakes at the town bakery. Gabby was going to bring chicken wings and another dessert. Her mother always brought her famous potato salad and macaroni salad. Several steaks would be seared on the grill and sliced up along with kielbasa.

Cliff was bringing apple cider which Sage would put in a large pot with orange slices and cinnamon sticks and let simmer on the stove. The smell alone would make the house feel festive. His mother also offered to make a homemade apple crisp and fresh whipped cream.

She didn't know what any of the other guests would bring if they popped in for a visit. Sometimes some of her clients showed up to wish everyone a Merry Christmas, stayed for a drink and then left. It was an open invitation to an open house but not on such a grand scale as the Flemming family's was. Sage and her mom, Sarah, were well liked in town and people showed up for the Christmas party on Christmas Eve where Christmas Day was more personal.

You guys are going to have to stay upstairs tonight," she said to the cats. "I don't want you sneaking out the door and go missing at night with the coyotes out there."

The steaks were laid on a platter and seasoned on both sides. The kielbasa was sliced in half and set on the same platter. While the eggs were cooking, Sage rewrapped the torn gifts and wrapped the new ones. The tree looked full and festive and would look even better once everyone brought their gifts to be exchanged.

She returned to the kitchen, stuffed the deviled eggs, and sprinkled them with paprika. It was almost five o'clock.

"Where did the time go?" she asked the cats, stirring the meatballs. "I'll feed you supper now so I can take you upstairs with me when I change."

While the cats ate, Sage placed a bright red tablecloth on her drop-leaf table in the living room and set up the bar. The liquor bottles were lined up in the back and various sized plastic glasses were set in front of them. One side had an ice bucket full of ice cubes and the mixers. The other end of the table held a tray with olives, lemon wedges, lime wedges, orange slices, and cherries. The wine and beer were chilling in the fridge.

"Come on, guys, it's time for you to go upstairs."

She corralled the cats in her bedroom and closed the door so they couldn't get out again. Sage changed into her green velour pantsuit with green satin pumps. She wanted to be comfortable and enjoy herself, so she chose not to wear a dress.

"You be good," she said to the cats who had curled up on the bed with their full stomachs. "I'll be up to let you out a little later when things settle down."

Sage lit the Sterno under the warmer. She preheated the oven and then popped in the pigs in a blanket to cook. It was a little past six and her guests would be starting to arrive. The hot dishes would stay in the kitchen and the cold dishes would be set on the dining room table along with the plates, napkins, and silverware.

"Merry Christmas!" Gabby yelled from the front door.

"I'm in the kitchen," Sage replied.

Gabby and Rory were loaded down with food.

"Where do you want everything?" Rory asked. "I have to go back to the car and get the gifts."

"Just set them on the kitchen table and I'll sort where things go," Sage said. "You can hang your coats in the mud room."

Gabby was busy helping Sage put out the food when Cliff arrived along with Sage's mom. The food was piling up fast and Sage was running out of room in the fridge. The dining room table was full, and any desserts were put on a smaller table set up next to the bar.

"Have you heard from the sheriff?" Sage asked her mom.

"I did. He got home at six and said he'd be over shortly. I guess he had his hands full interrogating Stephen today. The kid is a loose cannon."

"Does he think Stephen did it?"

"I guess Stephen threw his brother under the bus and afterwards accused his mother and the butler of working together to do it. Gerald never did get a straight answer out of the kid."

"Is he in jail or at home for Christmas?" Sage asked.

"Really?" Gabby said, coming into the kitchen. "Do you have to talk about murder on Christmas Eve?"

"I was just asking a few questions," Sage said, defending herself. "Geez!"

"Who wants shrimp cocktail?" Sheriff White asked from the deck slider. "Happy Holidays!"

"Yum! Shrimp cocktail. Did you bring any cocktail sauce with you?" Sarah asked.

"A whole tub of it. You want it in the kitchen?"

"Yes, please," Sage answered. "Merry Christmas!"

"I need a drink after today. Maybe two or three," he replied, shaking his head. "Where do the gifts go?"

"Gerald, you didn't have to bring gifts," Sarah told her friend.

"I've never had to buy presents before this year, so you people are the lucky ones I get to try my gift giving skills out on. Ella always did the shopping, but I think she'd be proud of how well I did on my own this year."

"I'm sure she would," Sarah said, taking the bag of gifts from her friend. "I'll take care of these, you make a plate, after you get yourself a drink of course."

"What is that huge thing hidden behind the tree?" Sarah asked, returning from the living room.

Sage looked around to see if Cliff was anywhere near.

"It's Cliff's gift from me," she told her mother. "Wait until you see it."

"I think all the food is out. It's time to start this party," Sarah said.

The next couple of hours were spent eating, drinking, telling stories, and laughing, lots of laughing. People stopped in for a visit and dropped off small gifts of food or liquor adding to Sage's already well stocked bar. By ten o'clock it was just the close group of friends sitting in the living room talking.

"I think we need to exchange gifts," Gabby said.

"Sounds good to me," Cliff said. "I'm dying to know what's under the green blanket and who it's for."

"Unfortunately, I think you'll have a wait before you get to see what's there as all the other gifts are piled up in front of it," Sarah, said, laughing.

"That is unfortunate," Cliff replied, chuckling.

Gifts were exchanged and there were smiles all around. Cliff finally got to open his gift. He was extremely pleased with his sign but had to explain to Sarah and the sheriff what it was for and asked them to please keep the tree farm a secret until the official unveiling. Under the tree was finally empty and people were packing up to go home. No one noticed there was no gift from Cliff to Sage except for Sage. She let it go and didn't say anything.

Sage was in the kitchen wrapping food for people to take home with them and trying to find room in the fridge for the rest of it. The sheriff came in looking for a few more deviled eggs before they were put away. He filled a plate for a third time and started to eat.

"I don't get to eat like this at home. I usually make soup or a frozen dinner for supper and head to bed because the house is so quiet."

"You're welcome to come here any time for supper. Cliff is here almost every night and cooking for one more would not be a problem," Sage said, smiling.

"I appreciate that," he replied. "You and your mom think alike. She invited me over, too."

"Now that no one else is around I can ask how the interviews went today with the Flemmings," Sage said.

"Everyone was cooperative with the exception of Stephen. He's hiding something and I can't figure out what it is."

"He either did it or knows who did," Sage replied. "Did he blame his mother and the butler again?"

"He did, and I think he's trying to pin this on her, so he and his brother have free reign of the family fortune. She has always been the disciplinarian and now things will totally change with her in charge, and they won't have their father around to run interference."

"Do you think Mrs. Flemming killed her husband?"

"No, not at all. I don't think the butler did it either. They freely admitted they had been seeing each other for over ten years while Mr. Flemming had his various affairs. They stayed together but led separate lives. Weird, huh?"

"I guess you never know what goes on behind closed doors," Sage replied.

"I have the pictures of the crime scene with me. Do you want to look at them?" the sheriff asked.

"Absolutely!"

"I'll be right back," the sheriff said, setting down his plate and running out to his cruiser.

"Are you two at it again? You can't even take a break for Christmas Eve?" Gabby asked, setting down several bags she was carrying. "What are you looking at as if I didn't know?"

"Crime scene photos," Sage replied.

"There are four folders. One is photos taken in the parlor, one holds the den pictures, and the other two are the sons' bedrooms. I've looked them over but haven't seen anything I would deem suspicious."

Cliff, Rory, and Sarah joined them in the kitchen, all looking over the photos.

"The sons' rooms are a mess. You wouldn't expect that when they have maids," Gabby said.

"Mrs. Flemming apologized about the condition of their rooms. She said the maids are not allowed in there to clean as her sons want their privacy," the sheriff said.

"What is that under the cabinet?" Sage asked, handing the photo to the sheriff.

"I don't know. We didn't notice it when we were in the room," he admitted.

"Where are the photos of Stephen's room?" Sage asked.

The folder was handed to her, and she flipped through the pictures stopping on one in particular.

"Do you remember what Cora Ripple said when we dug her out of the bushes?"

"She said they were fighting over marshmallows," Cliff replied. "Why?"

"Look in this picture and tell me what looks like marshmallows in that picture taken in Stephen's room," Sage said. "What if they weren't fighting over a bag of marshmallows but one of the two people just happened to be holding something that looked like them from a distance?"

"What is that?" Cliff asked, pointing to the waste basket.

"I believe it is a bag of cotton balls," Sage answered. "And if you look at the picture in the parlor it looks like a cotton ball with a red discoloration on it under the cabinet."

"It does look like a cotton ball," the sheriff admitted.

"Gabby, what do you use cotton balls for at your salon?"

"We use them mostly for removing nail polish," she replied.

"What if whoever killed and moved Mr. Fleeming didn't realize they left the red marks on his clothes but did see nail polish on the murder weapon and tried to clean it before they buried it in the plant?"

"I need to get to the mansion before someone else finds the item under the cabinet and gets rid of it," the sheriff stated.

"Right after Stephen tried to attack me, there was someone standing in the front foyer listening to us. There were two maids, one of which was wearing bright red nail polish. What if she helped Stephen after he killed his father? Cora did say she saw two people standing in the room."

"I have to get to the mansion. Can I leave all my things here and get them tomorrow?"

"Sure. Text me and let me know if it's still there. I'll be up for a while yet," Sage requested.

Gabby and Rory followed right behind the sheriff. They said they would be there the following day to help with the meal preparation after they attended their family gatherings. Sage, her mom, and Cliff were the only ones left at the house. She went up to let the cats out of her bedroom. They tore down the stairs and right into the kitchen to get their dry food.

"You'd think I didn't feed them earlier," Sage said, rolling her eyes.

"I'll be over sometime after noon," Sarah said, hugging her daughter. "This was a wonderful night and I'm so glad Gerald was here with friends, even if he had to leave so suddenly."

"That cotton ball could be a crucial piece of evidence. Especially if they can match the nail polish on it, if that's what it is, to the same polish the maid was wearing," Sage replied.

"Have I ever told you how proud I am of you and your keen mind?"

"Many times, Mom," Sage said, smiling. "Merry Christmas and I'll see you tomorrow."

"I'm glad we saved opening up everyone's stockings for tomorrow. I love to see the funny gag gifts people get. Wait until you see what I put in the one I did," Sarah said, opening the door.

"What a night," Sage said as Cliff wrapped his arms around her waist. "It was nice to see everyone who stopped in. I guess word got out that I like Irish Cream because I now have six bottles of it."

"I want to thank you for the beautiful sign. The hunter green color with the goldleaf letters is going to look so cool over the entrance of the tree farm. I can't wait for my parents to see it."

"I'm glad you like it. I swore Mr. Stump to secrecy, and he promised not to breathe a word to anyone."

Sage's cell went off. The sheriff messaged her that the item was still there, and it indeed was a cotton ball with red polish on it. He brought Stephen and the maid with the red polish in for questioning even though it was Christmas Eve. Her son begged his mother to stay home but she sided with the sheriff. He ended by saying he would see her tomorrow.

Sage finished cleaning up the kitchen and poured herself a mug of hot cider from the pot on the stove. She offered one to Cliff and they went into the living room to sit on the couch in front of the tree. The cats jumped up with them and settled in.

"I'm curious. All night while people were opening their gifts, you never once said anything about me not getting you one," Cliff said, pulling her in close.

"You weren't obligated to get me a gift. I give Christmas presents because it makes me happy. If I receive one back that's fine, if I don't, that's fine, too."

"Wait here," he said, disappearing out the deck slider and returning with a good-sized box. "It's our first Christmas together, you didn't seriously think I would forget to get you a gift, did you?"

"I figured if you did, you were waiting for Christmas Day instead of tonight. Like I said, I don't look to receive gifts, but it's nice when I do," she admitted.

"Open it," Cliff said.

Sage started to unwrap it. She opened the box and inside was another wrapped box. This went on for nine boxes until she reached a small ring box in the last one. She looked at Cliff hoping it wasn't an engagement ring. They hadn't even been going out for a year and it was way too early for anything like that.

"Go ahead, open it," he said, smiling.

Inside, a beautiful ring with a deep purple amethyst center stone was surrounded by a ring of small diamonds. It was set in sterling silver.

"I know your favorite color is purple. It's not an engagement ring, just a friendship ring or maybe even a promise ring," he said, taking the ring out of its box. "I promise to wait and enjoy our life as it is right now and always be there if you need me to be."

He slid the ring on the ring finger of her right hand. It fit perfectly.

"How did you know my ring size?"

"You and your mom take the same size. I asked her and she helped me pick out a ring for you at *All That Glitters*."

"She knew all night and never let on. What a sneak," Sage said, holding her hand up in front of her to admire her gift. "Thank you, it's beautiful."

"You're beautiful," he whispered, pulling her in close again.

They refilled their hot cider and spent a little time snuggling before Cliff left for home. Sage locked up the house and went to bed. She lay there, staring at her ring, knowing what a great life she had.

CHAPTER FIVE

Christmas Day greeted Sage with a flurry of snow. She checked the weather to make sure the storm would not get any worse and that she'd have to cancel her Christmas plans. It was supposed to let up by noon and become just scattered flurries here and there.

The cats were fed, and Sage was enjoying her morning cup of coffee. Every time she took a drink her new ring caught her eye and made her smile.

"I wonder if Gabby knew about my ring?" she asked the cats. "People sure can keep secrets around here at Christmas time."

Sage dug her big roast pan out of the pantry. It was only used on Christmas Day so by the time the holiday rolled around the pan had always become buried at the back of the pantry. She washed it out and set the large side of prime rib in the pan. She seasoned it well, poured some water in the bottom of the pan, and covered it with foil. Setting the oven on a low setting, the meat would cook slowly leaving the center rare the way it was supposed to be served.

She made a green bean casserole and set it on the rack above the meat in the oven. A large pot of potatoes was set on top of the stove ready to be boiled for mashed potatoes at a later hour. Gabby was bringing her sweet potatoes with marshmallows and her mother was bringing mashed turnip, peas, and winter squash.

They still had plenty of desserts from the previous night, but to be on the safe side, Sage had bought an apple pie, a banana cream pie, and blueberry pie to finish the dinner. She had eggnog, tomato juice, and wine to be served at dinner.

Sage set all the stockings under the tree where the gifts had been the night before. She retrieved her good porcelain China from the corner cabinet and set the table for ten people. Christmas dinner was one of Sage's favorite times of the year and this year Cliff and his parents had been added to the mix. Dinner was scheduled for four o'clock giving people enough time to visit with other family and friends.

This time, Smokey and Motorboat would be allowed to stay downstairs as once everyone was there for dinner, other unexpected guests wouldn't be showing up and going in and out enabling the cats to run out the door. They were happy because Cliff's big sign was gone, and they could get up in the bay window again. The cats were batting at the falling snowflakes through the window when Sarah first arrived.

Sage helped her get all the food inside she had brought with her. The vegetables were already cooked and would only have to be heated up in the microwave prior to eating. They sat in the living room together having a glass of wine. They talked about Sage's ring and how Cliff had bought it weeks ago and kept it a secret.

The others started to trickle in. They made drinks and sat in the living room talking. Cliff took the roaster pan out of the oven and put the slab of meat on a cutting board to let it rest. Everyone was there but the sheriff and it was almost four.

"Does anyone mind if we give Gerald another half an hour before we start eating?" Sarah asked.

Everyone agreed by a nod of the head to wait a little while longer for the sheriff.

"The sign you gave Cliff is great and will look good on the farm," Mr. Fulton said to Sage. "I can't wait to get the project up and running. We got the okay on the last soil report to get started. We'll start in the spring."

"That's exciting," Sarah replied. "How long do you think it will be before the first batch of trees will be ready to sell?"

"It will be a few years before that happens. We will plant new trees each year to keep the crops rotating and have new trees each year to sell," Cliff stated.

"Sage, don't you just love your ring?" Gabby asked.

"You knew about it, too?" Sage asked her. "Some best friend you are keeping secrets from me."

"It wasn't just me, everyone knew and kept it a secret," Gabby said in her own defense.

"Mom, do you want to help me start to get the food on the table? Cliff, can you carve the prime rib into one-inch slabs, please?"

Everything was on the table. At the last second the sheriff pulled into the driveway and rushed through the slider apologizing for being late and holding dinner up. He grabbed a beer out of the fridge and they all sat down. As people were filling their plates, Sage spoke up.

"Are you going to keep us in suspense? What happened with Stephen and the maid?" Sage asked.

"It was amazing. We brought them down to the station and put them in separate rooms. I was with Stephen and Bell was in with the maid."

"But did you find out who killed Mr. Flemming?" Gabby asked.

"We did. The maid killed him out of anger, but she wouldn't own up to anything at first. She hadn't planned on doing it. She lost her temper and grabbed the statue and whacked him with it. Stephen helped her hide the body."

"But why did she do it, and why would Stephen blame his mother if he knew someone else did it?" Sage asked.

"Stephen and the maid were dating, and I guess it was pretty serious. She overheard the parent's conversation about making the boys go into the military and saw her way to an easy life slipping through her fingers if Stephen left."

"So, if he blamed his mother and they found her guilty he could stay with his girlfriend and have all the family money," Cliff replied.

"The maid went into the den to talk to Mr. Flemming about Stephen staying out of the military so they could get married. He laughed at her, walked away heading toward the parlor, and she followed him. He informed her that even if his son didn't go into the military there would be no way he would let him marry a maid. She was furious and grabbed the statue and popped him one."

"What about the cotton balls?" Sarah asked.

"She had just done her nails and thought they were dry, but they weren't. When she grabbed the angel, red polish was transferred to the statue. She tried to wipe it off with her fingers but made more of a mess. So, she grabbed the bag of cotton balls and the polish remover out of the bathroom and cleaned off the statue. She thought she had gathered all of the ones she used but one dropped and landed under the cabinet."

"And she just confessed all this to you?" Sage asked.

"Oh, no. When I told Stephen he was going to be charged with the murder of his father because the cotton balls were found in his room and there was a witness who saw the two of them with the bag of cotton balls, he started to, as they say, sing like a bird. He admitted to helping her put the body in the cabinet but insists his father was dead by the time she came to get him for help. He turned on her big time to save himself. It was only when Bell told the maid Stephen had told the whole story, she broke down crying and made a statement."

"Will Stephen be charged with anything?" Sarah asked.

"Some lesser charges. Obstructing justice, hindering an investigation, and concealing a body, but he won't be charged with murder," the sheriff replied. "I'm sure his mother will hire a good attorney for him who will get him off on probation."

"More than likely," Mr. Fulton said.

"But if it hadn't been for Sage seeing the cotton ball under the cabinet and the bag of them in Stephen's waste basket, we might not have solved this."

"It wasn't me; it was Mrs. Ripple who solved this one. I only put two and two together, but she was the one who saw the bag of cotton balls before she fell into the bushes," Sage admitted.

"Now can we forget about the Flemmings and enjoy Christmas dinner," Gabby asked.

"We can, at least until tomorrow when I have to go back over there and collect the cabinet and the unused raffle gifts," Sage said, reaching for the open bottle of wine in the center of the table. "LouAnn, we have a great start for next year with all the gifts Mrs. Flemming has donated."

"We'll have to have a wine tasting party after the new year so we can get together and open all the gifts, so we know what's in them. I'll have to send Marion a thank you note. She does so much for the families of Cupston."

The conversation took a lighter turn. After dinner they all retired to the living room to open stockings. Each person walked forward and picked a full stocking from under the tree. Once everyone had a stocking, the gifts inside them were opened. There was a lot of laughter at the gag gifts each one contained. The sheriff got the stocking Sage filled and was quite happy with all the nips contained in it. There was also a bundle of gum with a note on it to chew after drinking to hide the alcohol breath. In the toe was a get out of jail free card in case you got pulled over. The sheriff said he would set the card on his desk at work.

Pie and coffee ended the night. Mr. and Mrs. Fulton were the first ones to leave, followed by Gabby's parents. Gabby helped her friend clean up the kitchen and dining room table before her and Rory left for the evening.

Sarah packed up some food for Flora and her fiancé which she would give her employee the following day at work. Cliff took all her belongings out to her car. The sheriff was going to follow Sarah home to make sure she made it okay on the slippery roads.

"This was a wonderful Christmas," Sarah said, hugging her daughter. "Good food, good friends, and good times."

"We are so lucky, Mom. I don't think it gets any better than what we have right now," Sage replied, hugging her tightly.

"Thank you for my ring. I can't wait to show Flora tomorrow. You hold on to that guy of yours. He's a one in a million catch," Sarah whispered as Cliff returned to the house.

"Thank you for everything," the sheriff said, holding up a bag full of food to take home with him. "I was going to sit home all weekend and eat frozen dinners and watch television. This was so much better. If you have any problem at the Flemming's house tomorrow, don't hesitate to call me. Again, thank you."

The couple watched the two cars exit the driveway and disappear into the white blanket of snow that was falling. Sage closed the mud room door.

"I hope your parents enjoyed themselves," she said, cutting another piece of apple pie. "Do you want a piece? I'm going to heat it up in the microwave and then load it with vanilla ice cream."

"I can do with another piece of pie and yes, my parents really enjoyed themselves."

"Do you want to build a fire while I fix our pie?"

"One blazing fire coming up," Cliff replied. "If it gets too cozy in here I might not want to drive home in the storm."

Cliff was sitting on the couch watching the fire when Sage handed him his pie and sat down next to him. The cats liked the warmth of the fire and curled up on the hearth rug in front of the fireplace screen.

"Good catch on the cotton ball last night," he said in between bites of pie.

"Lucky is more like it," she replied.

"Luck nothing. You're good at that kind of stuff, solving mysteries, I mean."

"I do enjoy a good mystery," she admitted. "How did you like spending Christmas with my family and our traditions?"

"I want to do it every year."

"I think that can be arranged, Mr. Fulton," she said, kissing his cheek. "And if you were serious about not driving home in the storm, I do have the spare room upstairs."

"This is the best Christmas ever," he said.

ALSO BY DONNA CLANCY

Check out all the books in Donna Clancy's catalog!

Donna Clancy Book Catalog

AUTHOR'S NOTE

I'd love to hear your thoughts on my books, the storylines, and anything else that you'd like to comment on—reader feedback is very important to me. My contact information, along with some other helpful links, is listed on the next page. If you'd like to be on my list of "folks to contact" with updates, release and sales notifications, etc.… just shoot me an email and let me know. Thanks for reading!

Also…

… if you're looking for more great reads, Summer Prescott Books publishes several popular series by outstanding Cozy Mystery authors.

CONTACT SUMMER PRESCOTT BOOKS PUBLISHING

Blog and Book Catalog: http://summerprescottbooks.com
Email: summer.prescott.cozies@gmail.com

And…be sure to check out the Summer Prescott Cozy Mysteries fan page and Summer Prescott Books Publishing Page on Facebook – let's be friends!

To sign up for our fun and exciting newsletter, which will give you opportunities to win prizes and swag, enter contests, and be the first to know about New Releases, click here: http://summerprescottbooks.com

Printed in Great Britain
by Amazon

35901716R00067